E
F/o
c/
Decatur/WF

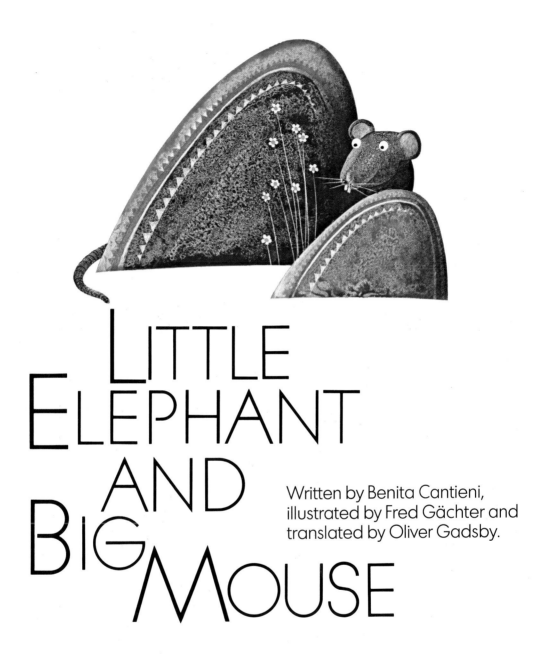

LITTLE ELEPHANT AND BIG MOUSE

Written by Benita Cantieni,
illustrated by Fred Gächter and
translated by Oliver Gadsby.

NEUGEBAUER PRESS, U.S.A.

The little elephant lives in a place
where lots of trees and flowers grow.
Most mornings he is awakened early
by the huge yellow sun.

But when it rains, he sleeps late into the day.
When the sun is hidden behind gray clouds
he almost forgets that there are ever sunny days.
However, since he's an elephant, he doesn't quite forget,
and he likes to dream about all the wonderful things
he has seen in the world.

The little elephant is very young,
and he hasn't grown as fast
as the other young elephants.
That's why he's called Little Elephant.
The other elephants don't invite him
to play very often.

Little Elephant still has plenty of friends, though –
friends of all different shapes and sizes.
Most of them are smaller than he is,
but he's very fond of them all, and they like him.

His best friend is the big mouse.
He is the same age as Little Elephant,
but he's grown much faster than the other mice.
That's why he's called Big Mouse.

Big Mouse is too small to play elephant games,
and Little Elephant is way too big for mouse games.
Sometimes this makes the two friends very unhappy.

When they go for walks Little Elephant often takes Big Mouse on his back. The mouse is very curious and he keeps asking the elephant questions. "What would happen if someone stole the world?" asks Big Mouse. "No one can steal the world. It's too big," says the elephant. "In fact, it's enormous."

"But how big is it?" Big Mouse wants to know.
"Look, I'll show you." says Little Elephant.
"You see that big blue flower
 with the tiny white dot on it?
 If we pretend that the flower is the world,
 then I would be the little dot.
 And you are so much smaller than I am –
 why, we couldn't even see you."

Big Mouse thinks hard about this for a while –
so hard that deep furrows appear on his forehead.
"Why couldn't we see me on the world?
I'm a big mouse – everyone says so!"

"Of course you're big," says the elephant.
"But you're a mouse and even the biggest mouse
 is small on the world, because mice are small animals,
 and the world is so large."
"Oh, I see," says the mouse, "But It's still funny that
 everyone calls you a little elephant and me a big mouse,
 when you are so much bigger than I am."

"Is the sun smaller than the world?"
asks the curious mouse.

"No, it only looks smaller," explains the elephant, "because the sun is so far away.
The difference in size between the sun and the world is even bigger than the difference between us."

Little Elephant enjoys explaining things.
And Big Mouse is very glad to know
that the world and the sun are so big.
So big, in fact, that no one can steal them.

All this thinking and talking has made
Little Elephant and Big Mouse very tired.
So, full of contentment,
they lie down among the flowers
and fall asleep in the bright sunshine.

Copyright © 1981, Verlag Neugebauer Press, Salzburg, Austria.
Original title: Der kleine Elefant und die große Maus
Copyright © 1982, English text, Neugebauer Press U.S.A. Inc., Boston.
Published in U.S.A. by Neugebauer Press U.S.A. Inc., Distribution by Alphabet Press, Boston.
Distributed in Canada by Grolier Ltd., Toronto.
All rights reserved.
ISBN 0-907234-09-7
Printed in Austria